ENTER THE DOJO!

MARTIAL ARTS FOR KIDS

AIKIDO

DAVID KLIMCHUK

PowerKiDS
press

New York

Published in 2020 by The Rosen Publishing Group, Inc.
29 East 21st Street, New York, NY 10010

First Edition

Editor: Greg Roza
Book Design: Reann Nye

Photo Credits: Series art Reinhold Leitner/Shutterstock.com; cover, pp. 5, 14, 18, 22 Master1305/Shutterstock.com; p. 6 https://en.wikipedia.org/wiki/File:Morihei_Ueshiba_Portrait.jpg; p. 7 Keystone/Hulton Archive/Getty Images; p. 9 Artyom Geodakyan/TASS/Getty Images; p. 11 Ravil Sayfullin/Shutterstock.com; p. 13 Adam Crowley/Getty Imges; p. 15 Boris Ryaposov/Shutterstock.com; p. 17 Kzenon/Shutterstock.com; p. 19 recep-bg/E+/Getty Images; p. 21 MoMo Productions/DigitalVision/Getty Images.

Library of Congress Cataloging-in-Publication Data

Names: Klimchuk, David, author.
Title: Aikido / David Klimchuk.
Description: New York : PowerKids Press, [2020] | Series: Enter the dojo!
  martial arts for kids | Includes index.
Identifiers: LCCN 2019017339| ISBN 9781725309982 (pbk.) | ISBN 9781725310001
  (library bound) | ISBN 9781725309999 (6 pack)
Subjects: LCSH: Aikido–Juvenile literature.
Classification: LCC GV1114.35 .K57 2020 | DDC 796.815/4–dc23
LC record available at https://lccn.loc.gov/2019017339

Manufactured in the United States of America

The activities discussed and displayed in this book can cause serious injury when attempted by someone who is untrained in the martial arts. Never try to replicate the techniques in this book without the supervision of a trained martial arts instructor.

CPSIA Compliance Information: Batch #CWPK20. For Further Information contact Rosen Publishing, New York, New York at 1-800-237-9932.

CONTENTS

WHAT IS AIKIDO?. 4

THE HISTORY OF AIKIDO 6

WHO DOES AIKIDO? 8

IN THE DOJO. 10

STARTING CLASS 12

DURING CLASS 14

JOINT LOCKS 16

THROWS 18

BELTS AND RECOGNITION 20

CHANGING YOUR ENERGY. 22

GLOSSARY 23

INDEX. 24

WEBSITES. 24

What Is Aikido?

Aikido is a martial art that focuses on using the energy and movement of your **opponent** against them. In aikido, students don't learn how to throw punches or kicks. Instead, they're taught different throws and joint locks. This art isn't meant to be performed in competitions. Aikido is meant to beat not just your opponent but the **negative** energy in yourself.

The goal of aikido is to create peace and harmony in yourself and in the world! The word "aikido" is broken down into three Japanese words: "ai" meaning "harmony," "ki" meaning "energy," and "do" meaning "the way."

Kiai!

Many aikido **practitioners** practice with weapons such as the bokken, jo, and tanto, which are wooden versions of old Japanese weapons. Practicing with weapons helps improve timing and **stances** and develops the students' understanding of distance.

4

Aikido can be practiced by people of all ages and abilities.

The History of Aikido

Aikido is heavily **influenced** by another art known as jujitsu. Aikido was created by Morihei Ueshiba in Japan around 1942. After returning from the Russo-Japanese War, he spent many years training in **solitude**. Ueshiba is often referred to as "Osensei" or "great teacher." His picture hangs in all aikido schools.

MORIHEI UESHIBA

Kiai!

Ueshiba was more than just the founder of aikido. Throughout his life, he was known for standing up for the rights of low-income workers. He also taught that farming and martial arts were connected.

Morihei Ueshiba practiced and taught aikido up until a month before his death at age 85.

Ueshiba wanted to create a style of martial art that was less **aggressive** than jujitsu and caused fewer injuries. He wanted an art that focused more on fitness of the mind and less on causing harm to others. Ueshiba purposefully created aikido as a **defensive** martial art that includes very few attacks.

Who Does Aikido?

Those who practice aikido are known as aikidoka. Aikidoka practice aikido in schools called "dojos." These individuals commit to **rigorous** practice of the principles created by Ueshiba. Due to aikido being less focused on strikes and colorful fight scenes, this art is featured far less in movies and television than other more well-known arts such as kung fu or karate.

The most well-known aikidoka in the United States is Steven Seagal. He starred in *Above the Law*, which is the first American movie to include an aikido fight scene. American aikidoka Terry Dobson studied with Ueshiba and helped spread the popularity of aikido in the United States.

Steven Seagal has taught aikido all around the world. He is also a musician, actor, and police officer.

9

In the Dojo

When practicing aikido in the dojo, students are expected to wear a "gi," sometimes called an aikidogi or keikogi. Some dojos will loan first-time students a gi, but if you plan to continue your training, it's best to buy your own.

You are expected to bow as a sign of respect every time you enter or leave the dojo practice area. The first thing you see when you enter the dojo is the "shomen," which means "front" in Japanese. Here you will find a picture of Ueshiba and occasionally a picture of another aikidoka that your particular dojo finds important.

Kiai!

Etiquette is very important in aikido studios. For example, seasoned students and instructors may find it rude or offensive if you turn your back to the shomen or leave your bags near or along the front wall of the studio.

Students wearing aikido gis sit in seiza, or a seated position, before starting class.

11

Starting Class

Always try to get to your aikido class early so you can warm up. As class begins, students often sit in seiza in front of the instructor. When sitting in seiza, you are encouraged to relax and feel your worries drift away.

When the instructor arrives, the class stands up. The instructor and the students bow to the shomen, clap twice, bow again, then bow to each other. This act of respect happens at the beginning and end of each class.

During an aikido class, students are never just sitting or standing around! You are expected to be either exercising, practicing **techniques**, or listening to the instructor.

Before starting each class, students and instructors bow to a picture of Morihei Ueshiba located at the front of the dojo.

During Class

All aikido classes begin with stretches led by either the instructor or an advanced student. These stretches are called "aikitaiso" and last about 15 minutes. Warming up also includes general exercises, such as sit-ups and push-ups. During the warm-up period, students are expected to count to 10 in Japanese together.

Kiai!

"Tori" means "active partner," or the person practicing a technique. "Uke" means "the receiver of the technique," or the person who allows the tori to practice an aikido technique.

Most of class is spent learning and practicing techniques. For beginners, students practice falling and rolling. The instructor will show the proper form and then students break into pairs to train. The student practicing the technique is called the "tori," while the student attacking is known as the "uke."

Joint Locks

Aikido techniques are usually broken down into two kinds: joint locks and throws. A joint lock occurs when a joint is forced into a position that is uncomfortable or painful.

The first joint lock students learn is called ikkyo. Like most aikido techniques, it has many **variations**. Ikkyo is a defense against an attacker who grabs your wrist. The first step is to guide your opponent's hand up, and move them off their center of balance. Use the other hand to grab and lift their elbow while stepping toward them. This movement places pressure on the attacker's elbow joint, making it easier to throw them to the ground.

Kiai!

"Centering" is a fundamental principle in aikido. It's important to keep your center of balance so you can stay firmly on your feet. It's equally important to move your opponent away from their center of balance in order to throw them to the mat.

Ikkyo is an elbow lock. Other joint locks target the wrist or shoulder joints. Others rely on "pressure points," which are places on the body where force is particularly painful.

Throws

Once you have your opponent in a joint lock, it's common to use a throw to take them to the ground. Aikido throws can be very dangerous, so make sure you are practicing them under the eye of a trained sensei, or instructor.

Kiai!

Aikido techniques rely on directing movements. Irimi is a movement that enters or matches the opponent's movements and uses them against them. Tenkan is a pivot or quick turn used to redirect an opponent's movements.

By using their opponent's **momentum** against them, aikido practitioners can easily throw their opponents without needing much strength.

One common throw is irimi nage, which means "entering throw." This technique can be used against a variety of attacks including wrist grabs and strikes. Irimi nage starts with a quick spin to get your opponent off balance. The next move is to raise your arm and place it under the opponent's chin. By quickly spinning the other way, you can easily throw your opponent to the mat.

19

Belts and Recognition

Although many Western aikido schools have a belt system that includes many colors, aikido as taught by Osensei has degrees, or levels, known as "kyu." After students have mastered these degrees, they are given a black belt, which has 10 more degrees, known as "dan."

Movement from one degree to the next requires a certain number of practice days and mastery of certain techniques that you are required to perform in front of your sensei. Usually an advanced student is chosen to help you show your techniques.

Although not originally used in aikido, different colored belts can help encourage students, especially children and teens, to train harder and practice more.

Changing Your Energy

Now that you know a little bit about aikido, you can begin your journey as an aikidoka! Just remember that aikido techniques can be dangerous, especially for beginners. Be sure to practice safely and under the guidance of an expert.

Unlike many martial arts, aikido is a defensive martial art. It is great for self-defense. Aikido training takes **discipline** and hard work, but it's also rewarding. You will learn to control your body's movements, but also the negative energy within and around you. As a result, you will be doing your part to bring more positive energy to the world around you.

GLOSSARY

aggressive: The act of being bold and forceful toward others.

defensive: Having to do with keeping yourself safe.

discipline: A way of behaving that shows a willingness to obey rules or orders.

etiquette: Rules governing the proper way to behave or to do something.

influenced: To be impacted or changed by something.

momentum: The strength or force that something has when it is moving.

negative: Harmful, bad, or not wanted.

opponent: Someone competing against another person.

practitioner: Someone who practices a certain specialty.

rigorous: Very strict and demanding.

solitude: The act of being alone or away from others.

stance: The way someone stands.

technique: The manner in which physical movements are used for a particular purpose, such as training in a martial art.

variation: A form of something that is slightly different from other forms of the same thing.

23

INDEX

A

aikidoka, 8, 10, 15, 22
aikitaiso, 14

B

bokken, 4

C

centering, 16

D

dan, 20
Dobson, Terry, 8

G

gi, 10, 11

I

ikkyo, 16, 17
irimi nage, 19

J

jo, 4
joint lock, 4, 16, 17, 18
jujitsu, 6, 7

K

karate, 8
kung fu, 8
kyu, 20

O

Osensei, 6, 20

P

pressure point, 17

S

seiza, 11, 12
sensei, 18, 20
shomen, 10, 12

T

tanto, 4
throw, 4, 16, 18, 19
tori, 14, 15

U

Ueshiba, Morihei, 6, 7, 8,
     10, 13
uke, 14, 15

WEBSITES

Due to the changing nature of Internet links, PowerKids Press has developed an online list of websites related to the subject of this book. This site is updated regularly. Please use this link to access the list: www.powerkidslinks.com/ETD/aikido